Flabbergaster

Lee Aucoin, *Creative Director*
Jamey Acosta, *Senior Editor*
Heidi Fiedler, *Editor*
Produced and designed by
Denise Ryan & Associates
Illustration © Ed Myer
Rachelle Cracchiolo, *Publisher*

Teacher Created Materials

5301 Oceanus Drive
Huntington Beach, CA 92649-1030
http://www.tcmpub.com
Paperback: ISBN: 978-1-4333-5603-2
Library Binding: ISBN: 978-1-4807-1725-1
© 2014 Teacher Created Materials

SELECTED BY
MARK CARTHEW

ILLUSTRATED BY
ED MYER

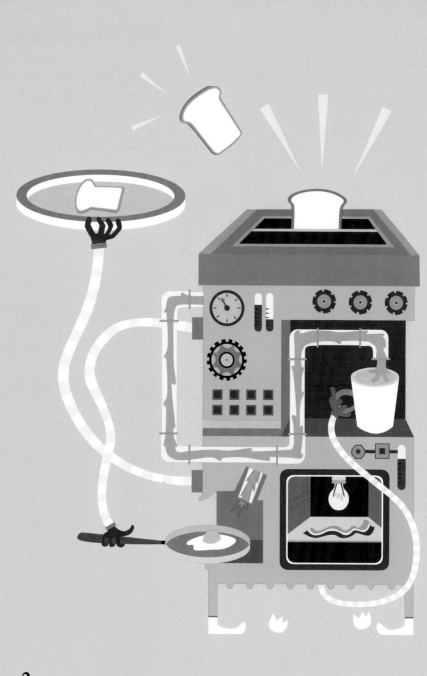

CONTENTS

CONSTRUCTION JOB

Crane, oh crane, your neck is long
And I have a song for the ground:
    Hook the girders,
    Rope the girders
    Hoist the girders round.

Crane, oh crane, your chain is strong
And I have a song for the skies:
    Bolt the girders,
    Weld the girders
    Watch the girders rise.

Myra Cohn Livingston

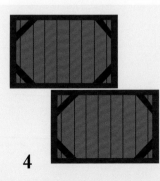

THE POWER SHOVEL

The power digger
Is much bigger
     Than the biggest beast I know.
He snorts and roars
Like the dinosaurs
     That lived long years ago.

He crouches low
     On his tractor paws
And scoops the dirt up
     With his jaws;
Then swings his long
     Stiff neck around
And spits it out
     Upon the ground.

Oh, the power digger
Is much bigger
    Than the biggest beast I know.
He snorts and roars
Like the dinosaurs
    That lived long years ago.

Rowena Bennett

OUR WASHING MACHINE

Our washing machine went whisity
        whirr
Whisity whisity whisity whirr
One day at noon it went whisity click
Whisity whisity whisity click
Click grr click grr click grr click
        Call the repairman
        Fix it…Quick!

Patricia Hubbell

INSINKERATOR®

Mashed potato
Grinding
Grater
Gobbled in
InSinkErator®

Mark Carthew

THE TOASTER

A silver scaled dragon with jaws flaming red

Sits at my elbow and toasts my bread.

I hand him fat slices, and then, one by one,

He hands them back when he sees
they are done.

William Jay Smith

THE DRONING DRAIN MACHINE

A curling
    twirling
    snaky coil
       creeps out
          from the drain unclogger
            it twirls and whirls
          like plumber's curls
            to free
          the pipe's
        bog sogger.
With a question mark
         it disappears...
            into the great unclean
         unwinding
      ever slowly
    from the droning
drain machine.

Heading
   down
      deep
        underground

the
steely
snake
descends,
coils
uncurling
round
and
round
past
tree roots,
dark
and
bends...

MUD
MUSH
SLIMY SLUDGE
BIG
BULGING
BOGGERS
BUDGE!

Mark Carthew

11

POWER TO THE BEATER

Nothing could be sweeter
than an electric beater
when its blades are turned on slow.
The goo slews and slobs
in delightful soft globs
and it sits in the bowl quite low.

But turn it on fast
and then what a blast
for the blades now whiz and whirr.
They're shrill and they squeak
in a high-pitched shriek
and the goo is just one blur.

And then with a quake
you make the mistake
of tilting the blades—quite small
and the goo starts to splatter
and you drop the lot and scatter
for the mixture's heading down the hall!

So beware with a beater,
for although there's nothing sweeter,
just think where a mixture can go.
And if you plan to hold it
to turn and gently fold it
then keep the blades switched on slow!

Janeen Brian

14

PEDAL POWER

While the school bus chugs around
It stops all over our small town
But the children inside
Would much rather ride
As fast as they'd like
On my ten seater pedal-powered bike.

R.L. Moore

THE SHINY DIPPLEDOPPLER

The shiny Dippledoppler
makes toast from thick sliced bread;
then pops it on a silver tray
served with your choice of spread.

Its program makes a hot drink fast
with every order taken.
Let's punch in number twenty-two…
for toast with eggs and bacon!

Mark Carthew

THE PIZZA OVEN

With a…
clicker
flicker
the oven ticker timer
trips the switch
on sixty second cycles
as the bakers
twirl and twitch.

Pizza pans
await their turn
for toppings piled in rows.
Salami, garlic,
Herbs and cheese—
Smells that tease the nose.

Tomato paste,
pineapple,
prawns and peppers too,
the electric pizza oven
pulls the pizza through.

Beads of sweat
roll slowly down
past the bakers' brow.

Waiting
for the
ticker's tock
to say...
it's ready now!

Mark Carthew

JEAN MACHINE

It clanks
It cranks
It steams
It seams.
It tumble dries
It dyes blue jeans.

It hems and cuffs
It sews in rows
It stitches zippers
fixes bows.

It measures
cuts
irons each day.
It packs in boxes
then...
      stacks away!

Mark Carthew

DIVE AND DIP

Rise and rip, dive and dip, leaning
backwards with the strain.
Rattling, roaring, upward soaring,
swirling, whirling in your brain.

Looping, lunging, downward
plunging, going round a dizzy bend.
Swinging, clinging, heads are ringing,
holding tightly to a friend.

Hands that clasp, scream and gasp,
funny feelings here inside.
Ears are popping, now we're stopping.

That's a roller coaster ride.

Max Fatchen

FLABBERGASTER

Little sister
Flabbergaster
Rode upon the roller coaster
"Faster, Faster!
I won't fluster!"
Cried my sister, silly boaster.

"Faster, faster!"
  Thus disaster
Happened on the roller coaster.
  Out flew sister
  Like a crust-a-
Pizza from a pop-up toaster.

Doug McLeod

MR. MAD'S MACHINE

Mr. Mad has made a machine
To take you round the world.
Its wheels are square. Its tail is long.
Its wings are thin and curled.

It blows out rings of purple smoke.
The engine squeaks and squeals.
The jets are very powerful.
They're made of cotton reels.

I wonder what it would be like
To fly in this machine?
It is the strangest sort of plane
That I have ever seen!

Tony Mitton

STEAM SHOVEL

The dinosaurs are not all dead.
I saw one raise its iron head
To watch me walking down the road
Beyond our house today.
Its jaws were dripping with a load
Of earth and grass that it had cropped.
It must have heard me where I
stopped,
Snorted white steam my way,
And stretched its long neck out to see,
And chewed, and grinned quite
amiably.

Charles Malam

SPARE PARTS

Nuts bolts
wrench socket
grease oil
spindle sprocket.
Anchor screws
tiny toggles
leather gloves
safety goggles.
Cranks cogs
Gears wheels
bucket teeth
rubber seals.
Pipes and tubes
hydraulic hoses
batteries pistons
rings and roses.

Bulky, bitsy, big or lean
nothing beats
a great machine!

Janeen Brian and Mark Carthew

Sources and Acknowledgments

Bennett, Rowena Bastin. "The Power Shovel" from The Day Is Dancing. Georgia: Modern Curriculum Press, Inc., 1948, 1968.

Brian, Janeen. "Power to the Beater" and "Spare Parts" from Machino Supremo! Poems About Machines. Victoria: Celapene Press, 2009.

Carthew, Mark. "InSinkErator®," "The Droning Drain Machine," "The Shiny Dippledoppler," "The Pizza Oven," and "The Jean Machine" from Machino Supremo! Poems About Machines. Victoria: Celapene Press, 2009.

Fatchen, Max. "Dive and Dip" from Peculiar Rhymes and Lunatic Lines. London: Orchard Books, 1995.

Hubbell, Patricia. "Our Washing Machine" from The Apple Vendor's Fair. New York: Atheneum Books, 1966.

Livingston, Myra Cohn . "Construction Job" from The Moon and a Star, and Other Poems. New York: Harcourt, Brace, and World, 1965. Reprinted by permission of Marian Reiner.

Malam, Charles. "Steam Shovel" from Upper Pasture. New York: Henry Holt and Company Inc., 1958.

McLeod, Doug. "Flabbergaster" from The Fed Up Family Album. Melbourne: Penguin Books Australia, 1983.

Mitton, Tony. "Mr. Mad's Machine" from Transport Poems. Oxford: Oxford University Press, 1994.

Moore, R.L. "Pedal Power." Copyright 2013. Published by permission of the author.

Smith, William Jay. "The Toaster" from Around My Room. New York: Farrar, Straus and Giroux, 2000.